The Gospel of Nature

Nature TEACHES

MORE THAN SHE

preaches. THERE

ARE NO *sermons*

IN *stones.*

John Burroughs

THE GOSPEL OF
Nature

AMERICAN ROOTS

Applewood Books
CARLISLE, MASSACHUSETTS

978-1-4290-9608-9

Cover and interior art © 2015 Noble Illustrations

"The Gospel of Nature" is a chapter from *Time and Change*
by John Burroughs. It was first published in 1912.

Thank you for purchasing an Applewood book.
Applewood reprints America's lively classics—
books from the past that are still of interest to modern readers.
Our mission is to build a picture of America's
past through its primary sources.

To inquire about this edition or to request a free copy
of our current catalog featuring our best-selling books, write to:
Applewood Books
P.O. Box 27
Carlisle, MA 01741
For more complete listings,
visit us on the web at:
www.awb.com

10 9 8 7 6 5 4 3 2 1

MANUFACTURED IN THE UNITED STATES OF AMERICA

The short works Applewood includes in its American Roots series have been selected to connect us. The books are tactile mementos of American passions by some of America's most famous writers. Each of these has meant something very personal to me.

I get little from religion. When my eldest son, Andy, died, I looked in vain for some word that would heal. Neither Western nor Eastern religions brought the teaching that I have found in a simple walk in the woods. Finding him and all the others I've lost on granite mountainsides, under gray clouds and blue skies, in snow and chilly downpours, on carpets of moss staring up into eternity, I am revived. And in the vibrant green fiddlehead unrolling in spring, the powder-blue robin's egg, and the dark down of a baby seagull, I am taught the future that was to be.

"*Nature teaches more than she preaches. There are no sermons in stones.*"

Phil Zuckerman
PUBLISHER

The other day a clergyman who described himself as a preacher of the gospel of Christ wrote, asking me to come and talk to his people on the gospel of Nature. The request set me to thinking whether or not Nature has any gospel in the sense the clergyman had in mind, any message that is likely to be specially comforting to the average orthodox religious person. I suppose the parson wished me to tell his flock what I had found in Nature that was a strength or a solace to myself.

What had all my many years of journeyings to Nature yielded me that would supplement or reinforce the gospel he was preaching? Had the birds taught me any valuable lessons? Had the four-footed beasts? Had the insects? Had the flowers, the trees, the soil, the coming and the going of the seasons? Had I really found sermons in stones, books in running brooks and good in everything? Had the lilies of the field, that neither toil nor spin, and yet are more royally clad than Solomon in all his glory, helped me in any way to clothe myself with humility, with justice, with truthfulness?

It is not easy for one to say just what he owes to all these things. Natural influences work indirectly as well as directly; they work upon the subconscious, as well as upon the conscious, self. That I am a saner, healthier, more contented man, with truer standards of life, for all my loiterings in the fields and woods, I am fully convinced.

That I am less social, less interested in my neighbors and in the body politic, more inclined to shirk civic and social responsibilities and to stop my ears against the brawling of the reformers, is perhaps equally true.

One thing is certain, in a hygienic way I owe much to my excursions to Nature. They have helped to clothe me with health, if not with humility; they have helped sharpen and attune all my senses; they have kept my eyes in such good trim that they have not failed me for one moment during all the seventy-five years I have had them; they have made my sense of smell so keen that I have much pleasure in the wild, open-air perfumes, especially in the spring—the delicate breath of the blooming elms and maples and willows, the breath of the woods, of the pastures, of the shore. This keen, healthy sense of smell has made me abhor tobacco and flee from close rooms, and put the stench of cities behind me. I fancy that this whole world of wild, natural perfumes is lost to the tobacco-user and to the city-dweller. Senses trained in the open air are in tune with open-air objects; they are quick, delicate, and discriminating. When I go to town, my ear suffers as well as my nose: the impact of the city upon my senses is hard and dissonant; the ear is stunned, the nose is outraged, and the eye is confused. When I come back, I go to Nature to be soothed and healed, and to have my senses put in tune once more. I know that, as a rule, country or farming folk are not remarkable for the delicacy of their senses, but this is owing mainly to the benumbing and brutalizing effect of continued hard labor. It is their minds more than their bodies that suffer.

When I have dwelt in cities the country was always near by, and I used to get a bite of country soil at least once a week to keep my system normal.

Emerson says that "the day does not seem wholly profane in which we have given heed to some natural object." If Emerson had stopped to qualify his remark, he would have added, if we give heed to it in the right spirit, if we give heed to it as a nature-lover and truth-seeker. Nature love as Emerson knew it, and as Wordsworth knew it, and as any of the choicer spirits of our time have known it, has distinctly a religious value. It does not come to a man or a woman who is wholly absorbed in selfish or worldly or material ends. Except ye become in a measure as little children, ye cannot enter the kingdom of Nature—as Audubon entered it, as Thoreau entered it, as Bryant and Amiel entered it, and as all those enter it who make it a resource in their lives and an instrument of their culture. The forms and creeds of religion change, but the sentiment of religion—the wonder and reverence and love we feel in the presence of the inscrutable universe—persists. Indeed, these seem to be renewing their life to-day in this growing love for all natural objects and in this increasing tenderness toward all forms of life. If we do not go to church so much as did our fathers, we go to the woods much more, and are much more inclined to make a temple of them than they were.

We now use the word Nature very much as our fathers used the word God, and, I suppose, back of it all we mean the power that is everywhere present and active, and in whose lap the visible universe is held and nourished. It is a power that we can see and touch and hear, and realize every moment of our lives how absolutely we are dependent upon it. There are no atheists or skeptics in regard to this power. All men see how literally we are its children, and all men learn how swift and sure is the penalty of disobedience to its commands.

Our associations with Nature vulgarize it and rob it of its divinity. When we come to see that the celestial and the terrestrial are one, that time and eternity are one, that mind and matter are one, that death and life are one, that there is and can be nothing not inherent in Nature, then we no longer look for or expect a far-off, unknown God.

Nature teaches more than she preaches. There are no sermons in stones. It is easier to get a spark out of a stone than a moral. Even when it contains a fossil, it teaches history rather than morals. It comes down from the fore-world an undigested bit that has resisted the tooth and maw of time, and can tell you many things if you have the eye to read them. The soil upon which it lies or in which it is imbedded was rock, too, back in geologic time, but the mill that ground it up passed the fragment of stone through without entirely reducing it. Very likely it is made up of the minute remains of innumerable tiny creatures that lived and died in the ancient seas. Very likely it was torn from its parent rock and brought to the place where it now lies by the great ice-flood that many tens of thousands of years ago crept slowly but irresistibly down out of the North over the greater part of all the northern continents.

But all this appeals to the intellect, and contains no lesson for the moral nature. If we are to find sermons in stones, we are to look for them in the relations of the stones to other things—when they are out of place, when they press down the grass or the flowers, or impede the plow, or dull the scythe, or usurp the soil, or shelter vermin, as do old institutions and old usages that have had their day. A stone that is much knocked about gets its sharp angles worn off, as do men. "A rolling stone gathers no moss," which is not bad for the stone, as moss hastens decay. "Killing two birds with one stone" is a bad saying, because it reminds boys to stone the birds, which is bad for both boys and birds. But "People who live in glass houses should not throw stones" is on the right side of the account, as it discourages stone-throwing and reminds us that we are no better than our neighbors.

The lesson in running brooks is that motion is a great purifier and health-producer. When the brook ceases to run, it soon stagnates. It keeps in touch with the great vital currents when it is in motion, and unites with other brooks to help make the river. In motion it soon leaves all mud and sediment behind. Do not proper work and the exercise of will power have the same effect upon our lives?

The other day in my walk I came upon a sap-bucket that had been left standing by the maple tree all the spring and summer. What a bucketful of corruption was that, a mixture of sap and rainwater that had rotted, and smelled to heaven. Mice and birds and insects had been drowned in it, and added to its unsavory character. It was a bit of Nature cut off from the vitalizing and purifying chemistry of the whole. With what satisfaction I emptied it upon the ground while I held my nose and saw it filter into the turf, where I knew it was dying to go and where I knew every particle of the reeking, fetid fluid would soon be made sweet and wholesome again by the chemistry of the soil!

II

I am not always in sympathy with nature-study as pursued in the schools, as if this kingdom could be carried by assault. Such study is too cold, too special, too mechanical; it is likely to rub the bloom off Nature. It lacks soul and emotion; it misses the accessories of the open air and its exhilarations, the sky, the clouds, the landscape, and the currents of life that pulse everywhere.

I myself have never made a dead set at studying Nature with note-book and field-glass in hand. I have rather visited with her. We have walked together or sat down together, and our intimacy grows with the seasons. What I have learned about her ways I have learned easily, almost unconsciously, while fishing or camping or idling about. My desultory habits have their disadvantages, no doubt, but they have their advantages also. A too strenuous pursuit defeats itself. In the fields and woods more than anywhere else all things come to those who wait, because all things are on the move, and are sure sooner or later to come your way.

To absorb a thing is better than to learn it, and we absorb what we enjoy. We learn things at school, we absorb them in the fields and woods and on the farm. When we look upon Nature with fondness and appreciation she meets us halfway and takes a deeper hold upon us than when studiously conned. Hence I say the way of knowledge of Nature is the way of love and enjoyment, and is more surely found in the open air than in the school-room or the laboratory. The other day I saw a lot of college girls dissecting cats and making diagrams of the circulation and muscle-attachments, and I thought it pretty poor business unless the girls were taking a course in comparative anatomy with a view to some occupation in life. What is the moral and intellectual value of this kind of knowledge to those girls? Biology is, no doubt, a great science in the hands of great men, but it is not for all. I myself have got along very well without it. I am sure I can learn more of what I want to know from a kitten on my knee than from the carcass of a cat in the laboratory. Darwin spent eight years dissecting barnacles; but he was Darwin, and did not stop at barnacles, as these college girls are pretty sure to stop at cats. He dissected and put together again in his mental laboratory the whole system of animal life, and the upshot of his work was a tremendous gain to our understanding of the universe.

I would rather see the girls in the fields and woods studying and enjoying living nature, training their eyes to see correctly and their hearts to respond intelligently. What is knowledge without enjoyment, without love? It is sympathy, appreciation, emotional experience, which refine and elevate and breathe into exact knowledge the breath of life. My own interest is in living nature as it moves and flourishes about me winter and summer.

I know it is one thing to go forth as a nature-lover, and quite another to go forth in a spirit of cold, calculating, exact science. I call myself a nature-lover and not a scientific naturalist. All that science has to tell me is welcome, is, indeed, eagerly sought for. I must know as well as feel. I am not merely contented, like Wordsworth's poet, to enjoy what others understand. I must understand also; but above all things I must enjoy. How much of my enjoyment springs from my knowledge I do not know. The joy of knowing is very great; the delight of picking up the threads of meaning here and there, and following them through the maze of confusing facts, I know well. When I hear the woodpecker drumming on a dry limb in spring or the grouse drumming in the woods, and know what it is all for, why, that knowledge, I suppose, is part of my enjoyment. The other part is the associations that those sounds call up as voicing the arrival of spring: they are the drums that lead the joyous procession.

To enjoy understandingly, that, I fancy, is the great thing to be desired. When I see the large ichneumon-fly, Thalessa, making a loop over her back with her long ovipositor and drilling a hole in the trunk of a tree, I do not fully appreciate the spectacle till I know she is feeling for the burrow of a tree-borer, Tremex, upon the larvae of which her own young feed. She must survey her territory like an oil-digger and calculate where she is likely to strike oil, which in her case is the burrow of her host Tremex. There is a vast series of facts in natural history like this that are of little interest until we understand them. They are like the outside of a book which may attract us, but which can mean little to us until we have opened and perused its pages.

The nature-lover is not looking for mere facts, but for meanings, for something he can translate into the terms of his own life. He wants facts, but significant facts—luminous facts that throw light upon the ways of animate and inanimate nature. A bird picking up crumbs from my window-sill does not mean much to me. It is a pleasing sight and touches a tender cord, but it does not add much to my knowledge of bird-life. But when I see a bird pecking and fluttering angrily at my window-pane, as I now and then do in spring, apparently under violent pressure to get in, I am witnessing a significant comedy in bird-life, one that illustrates the limits of animal instinct. The bird takes its own reflected image in the glass for a hated rival, and is bent on demolishing it. Let the assaulting bird get a glimpse of the inside of the empty room through a broken pane, and it is none the wiser; it returns to the assault as vigorously as ever.

The fossils in the rocks did not mean much to the earlier geologists. They looked upon them as freaks of Nature, whims of the creative energy, or vestiges of Noah's flood. You see they were blinded by the preconceived notions of the six-day theory of creation.

☙ III

I do not know that the bird has taught me any valuable lesson. Indeed, I do not go to Nature to be taught. I go for enjoyment and companionship. I go to bathe in her as in a sea; I go to give my eyes and ears and all my senses a free, clean field and to tone up my spirits by her "primal sanities." If the bird has not preached to me, it has added to the resources of my life, it has widened the field of my interests, it has afforded me another beautiful object to love, and has helped make me feel more at home in this world. To take the birds out of my life would be like lopping off so many branches from the tree: there is so much less surface of leafage to absorb the sunlight and bring my spirits in contact with the vital currents. We cannot pursue any natural study with love and enthusiasm without the object of it becoming a part of our lives. The birds, the flowers, the trees, the rocks, all become linked with our lives and hold the key to our thoughts and emotions.

Not till the bird becomes a part of your life can its coming and its going mean much to you. And it becomes a part of your life when you have taken heed of it with interest and affection, when you have established associations with it, when it voices the spring or the summer to you, when it calls up the spirit of the woods or the fields or the shore. When year after year you have heard the veery in the beech and birch woods along the trout streams, or the wood thrush May after May in the groves where you have walked or sat, and the bobolink summer after summer in the home meadows, or the vesper sparrow in the upland pastures where you have loitered as a boy or mused as a man, these birds will really be woven into the texture of your life.

What lessons the birds have taught me I cannot recall; what a joy they have been to me I know well. In a new place, amid strange scenes, theirs are the voices and the faces of old friends. In Bermuda the blue-birds and the catbirds and the cardinals seemed to make American territory of it. Our birds had annexed the island despite the Britishers.

For many years I have in late April seen the red-poll warbler, perhaps for only a single day, flitting about as I walked or worked. It is usually my first warbler, and my associations with it are very pleasing. But I really did not know how pleasing until, one March day, when I was convalescing from a serious illness in one of our sea-coast towns, I chanced to spy the little traveler in a vacant lot along the street, now upon the ground, now upon a bush, nervous and hurried as usual, uttering its sharp chip, and showing the white in its tail. The sight gave me a real home feeling. It did me more good than the medicine I was taking. It instantly made a living link with many past springs. Anything that calls up a happy past, how it warms the present! There, too, that same day I saw my first meadowlark of the season in a vacant lot, flashing out the white quills in her tail, and walking over the turf in the old, erect, alert manner. The sight was as good as a letter from home, and better: it had a flavor of the wild and of my boyhood days on the old farm that no letter could ever have.

The spring birds always awaken a thrill wherever I am. The first bobolink I hear flying over northward and bursting out in song now and then, full of anticipation of those broad meadows where he will soon be with his mate; or the first swallow twittering joyously overhead, borne on a warm southern breeze; or the first high-hole sounding out his long, iterated call from the orchard or field—how all these things send a wave of emotion over me!

Pleasures of another kind are to find a new bird, and to see an old bird in a new place, as I did recently in the old sugar-bush where I used to help gather and boil sap as a boy. It was the logcock, or pileated woodpecker, a rare bird anywhere, and one I had never seen before on the old farm. I heard his loud cackle in a maple tree, saw him flit from branch to branch for a few moments, and then launch out and fly toward a distant wood. But he left an impression with me that I should be sorry to have missed.

Nature stimulates our aesthetic and our intellectual life and to a certain extent our religious emotions, but I fear we cannot find much support for our ethical system in the ways of wild Nature. I know our artist naturalist, Ernest Thompson Seton, claims to find what we may call the biological value of the Ten Commandments in the lives of the wild animals; but I cannot make his reasoning hold water, at least not much of it. Of course the Ten Commandments are not arbitrary laws. They are largely founded upon the needs of the social organism; but whether they have the same foundation in the needs of animal life apart from man, apart from the world of moral obligation, is another question. The animals are neither moral nor immoral: they are unmoral; their needs are all physical. It is true that the command against murder is pretty well kept by the higher animals. They rarely kill their own kind: hawks do not prey upon hawks, nor foxes prey upon foxes, nor weasels upon weasels; but lower down this does not hold. Trout eat trout, and pickerel eat pickerel, and among the insects young spiders eat one another, and the female spider eats her mate, if she can get him. There is but little, if any, neighborly love among even the higher animals. They treat one another as rivals, or associate for mutual protection. One cow will lick and comb another in the most affectionate manner, and the next moment savagely gore her. Hate and cruelty for the most part rule in the animal world. A few of the higher animals are monogamous, but by far the greater number of species are polygamous or promiscuous. There is no mating or pairing in the great bovine tribe, and none among the rodents that I know of, or among the bear family, or the cat family, or among the seals. When we come to the birds, we find mating, and occasional pairing for life, as with the ostrich and perhaps the eagle.

As for the rights of property among the animals, I do not see how we can know just how far those rights are respected among individuals of the same species. We know that bees will rob bees, and that ants will rob ants; but whether or not one chipmunk or one flying squirrel or one wood mouse will plunder the stores of another I do not know. Probably not, as the owner of such stores is usually on hand to protect them. Moreover, these provident little creatures all lay up stores in the autumn, before the season of scarcity sets in, and so have no need to plunder one another. In case the stores of one squirrel were destroyed by some means, and it were able to dispossess another of its hoard, would it not in that case be a survival of the fittest, and so conducive to the well-being of the race of squirrels?

I have never known any of our wild birds to steal the nesting-material of another bird of the same kind, but I have known birds to try to carry off the material belonging to other species.

But usually the rule of might is the rule of right among the animals. As to most of the other commandments,—of coveting, of bearing false witness, of honoring the father and the mother, and so forth,—how can these apply to the animals or have any biological value to them? Parental obedience among them is not a very definite thing. There is neither obedience nor disobedience, because there are no commands. The alarm-cries of the parents are quickly understood by the young, and their actions imitated in the presence of danger, all of which of course has a biological value.

The instances which Mr. Seton cites of animals fleeing to man for protection from their enemies prove to my mind only how the greater fear drives out the lesser. The hotly pursued animal sees a possible cover in a group of men and horses or in an unoccupied house, and rushes there to hide. What else could the act mean? So a hunted deer or sheep will leap from a precipice which, under ordinary circumstances, it would avoid. So would a man. Fear makes bold in such cases.

I certainly have found "good in everything,"—in all natural processes and products,—not the "good" of the Sunday-school books, but the good of natural law and order, the good of that system of things out of which we came and which is the source of our health and strength. It is good that fire should burn, even if it consumes your house; it is good that force should crush, even if it crushes you; it is good that rain should fall, even if it destroys your crops or floods your land. Plagues and pestilences attest the constancy of natural law. They set us to cleaning our streets and houses and to readjusting our relations to outward nature. Only in a live universe could disease and death prevail. Death is a phase of life, a redistributing of the type. Decay is another kind of growth.

Yes, good in everything, because law in everything, truth in everything, the sequence of cause and effect in everything, and it may all be good to me if on the right principles I relate my life to it. I can make the heat and the cold serve me, the winds and the floods, gravity and all the chemical and dynamical forces, serve me, if I take hold of them by the right handle. The bad in things arises from our abuse or misuse of them or from our wrong relations to them. A thing is good or bad according as it stands related to my constitution. We say the order of nature is rational; but is it not because our reason is the outcome of that order? Our well-being consists in learning it and in adjusting our lives to it. When we cross it or seek to contravene it, we are destroyed. But Nature in her universal procedures is not rational, as I am rational when I weed my garden, prune my trees, select my seed or my stock, or arm myself with tools or weapons. In such matters I take a short cut to that which Nature reaches by a slow, roundabout, and wasteful process. How does she weed her garden? By the survival of the fittest. How does she select her breeding-stock? By the law of battle; the strongest rules. Hers, I repeat, is a slow and wasteful process. She fertilizes the soil by plowing in the crop. She cannot take a short cut. She assorts and arranges her goods by the law of the winds and the tides. She builds up with one hand and pulls down with the other. Man changes the conditions to suit the things. Nature changes the things to suit the conditions. She adapts the plant or the animal to its environment. She does not drain her marshes; she fills them up. Hers is the larger reason—the reason of the All. Man's reason introduces a new method; it cuts across, modifies, or abridges the order of Nature. I do not see design in Nature in the old ideological sense; but I see everything working to its own proper end, and that end is foretold in the means. Things are not designed; things are begotten. It is as if the final plan of a man's house, after he had begun to build it, should be determined by the winds and the rains and the shape of the ground upon which it stands. The eye is begotten by those vibrations in the ether called light, the ear by those vibrations in the air called sound, the sense of smell by those emanations called odors. There are probably other vibrations and emanations that we have no senses for because our well-being does not demand them.

We think it reasonable that a stone should fall and that smoke should rise because we have never known either of them to do the contrary. We think it reasonable that fire should burn and that frost should freeze, because this accords with universal experience. Thus, there is a large order of facts that are reasonable because they are invariable: the same effect always follows the same cause. Our reason is developed and disciplined by observing the order of Nature; and yet human rationality is of another order from the rationality of Nature. Man learns from Nature how to master and control her. He turns her currents into new channels; he spurs her in directions of his own. Nature has no economic or scientific rationality. She progresses by the method of trial and error. Her advance is symbolized by that of the child learning to walk. She experiments endlessly. Evolution has worked all around the horizon. In feeling her way to man she has produced thousands of other forms of life. The globe is peopled as it is because the creative energy was blind and did not at once find the single straight road to man. Had the law of variation worked only in one direction, man might have found himself the sole occupant of the universe. Behold the varieties of trees, of shrubs, of grasses, of birds, of insects, because Nature does not work as man does, with an eye single to one particular end. She scatters, she sows her seed upon the wind, she commits her germs to the waves and the floods. Nature is indifferent to waste, because what goes out of one pocket goes into another. She is indifferent to failure, because failure on one line means success on some other.

❧ IV

B*ut I am not preaching much* of a gospel, am I? Only the gospel of contentment, of appreciation, of heeding simple near-by things—a gospel the burden of which still is love, but love that goes hand in hand with understanding.

There is so much in Nature that is lovely and lovable, and so much that gives us pause. But here it is, and here we are, and we must make the most of it. If the ways of the Eternal as revealed in his works are past finding out, we must still unflinchingly face what our reason reveals to us. "Red in tooth and claw." Nature does not preach; she enforces, she executes. All her answers are yea, yea, or nay, nay. Of the virtues and beatitudes of which the gospel of Christ makes so much—meekness, forgiveness, self-denial, charity, love, holiness—she knows nothing. Put yourself in her way, and she crushes you; she burns you, freezes you, stings you, bites you, or devours you.

Yet I would not say that the study of Nature did not favor meekness or sobriety or gentleness or forgiveness or charity, because the great Nature students and prophets, like Darwin, would rise up and confound me. Certainly it favors seriousness, truthfulness, and simplicity of life; or, are only the serious and single-minded drawn to the study of Nature? I doubt very much if it favors devoutness or holiness, as those qualities are inculcated by the church, or any form of religious enthusiasm. Devoutness and holiness come of an attitude toward the universe that is in many ways incompatible with that implied by the pursuit of natural science. The joy of the Nature student like Darwin or any great naturalist is to know, to find out the reason of things and the meaning of things, to trace the footsteps of the creative energy; while the religious devotee is intent only upon losing himself in infinite being. True, there have been devout naturalists and men of science; but their devoutness did not date from their Nature studies, but from their training, or from the times in which they lived. Theology and science, it must be said, will not mingle much better than oil and water, and your devout scientist and devout Nature student lives in two separate compartments of his being at different times. Intercourse with Nature—I mean intellectual intercourse, not merely the emotional intercourse of the sailor or explorer or farmer—tends to beget a habit of mind the farthest possible removed from the myth-making, the vision-seeing, the voice-hearing habit and temper. In all matters relating to the visible, concrete universe it substitutes broad daylight for twilight; it supplants fear with curiosity; it overthrows superstition with fact; it blights credulity with the frost of skepticism. I say frost of skepticism advisedly. Skepticism is a much more healthful and robust habit of mind than the limp, pale-blooded, non-resisting habit that we call credulity.

In intercourse with Nature you are dealing with things at first hand, and you get a rule, a standard, that serves you through life. You are dealing with primal sanities, primal honesties, primal attraction; you are touching at least the hem of the garment with which the infinite is clothed, and virtue goes out from it to you. It must be added that you are dealing with primal cruelty, primal blindness, primal wastefulness, also. Nature works with reference to no measure of time, no bounds of space, and no limits of material. Her economies are not our economies. She is prodigal, she is careless, she is indifferent; yet nothing is lost. What she lavishes with one hand, she gathers in with the other. She is blind, yet she hits the mark because she shoots in all directions. Her germs fill the air; the winds and the tides are her couriers. When you think you have defeated her, your triumph is hers; it is still by her laws that you reach your end.

We make ready our garden in a season, and plant our seeds and hoe our crops by some sort of system. Can any one tell how many hundreds of millions of years Nature has been making ready her garden and planting her seeds?

There can be little doubt, I think, but that intercourse with Nature and a knowledge of her ways tends to simplicity of life. We come more and more to see through the follies and vanities of the world and to appreciate the real values. We load ourselves up with so many false burdens, our complex civilization breeds in us so many false or artificial wants, that we become separated from the real sources of our strength and health as by a gulf.

For my part, as I grow older I am more and more inclined to reduce my baggage, to lop off superfluities. I become more and more in love with simple things and simple folk—a small house, a hut in the woods, a tent on the shore. The show and splendor of great houses, elaborate furnishings, stately halls, oppress me, impose upon me. They fix the attention upon false values, they set up a false standard of beauty; they stand between me and the real feeders of character and thought. A man needs a good roof over his head winter and summer, and a good chimney and a big wood-pile in winter. The more open his four walls are, the more fresh air he will get, and the longer he will live.

How the contemplation of Nature as a whole does take the conceit out of us! How we dwindle to mere specks and our little lives to the span of a moment in the presence of the cosmic bodies and the interstellar spaces! How we hurry! How we husband our time! A year, a month, a day, an hour may mean so much to us. Behold the infinite leisure of Nature!

A few trillions or quadrillions of years, what matters it to the Eternal? Jupiter and Saturn must be billions of years older than the earth. They are evidently yet passing through that condition of cloud and vapor and heat that the earth passed through untold aeons ago, and they will not reach the stage of life till aeons to come. But what matters it? Only man hurries. Only the Eternal has infinite time. When life comes to Jupiter, the earth will doubtless long have been a dead world. It may continue a dead world for aeons longer before it is melted up in the eternal crucible and recast, and set on its career of life again.

Familiarity with the ways of the Eternal as they are revealed in the physical universe certainly tends to keep a man sane and sober and safeguards him against the vagaries and half-truths which our creeds and indoor artificial lives tend to breed. Shut away from Nature, or only studying her through religious fears and superstitions, what a mess a large body of mankind in all ages have made of it! Think of the obsession of the speedy "end of the world" which has so often taken possession of whole communities, as if a world that has been an eternity in forming could end in a day, or on the striking of the clock! It is not many years since a college professor published a book figuring out, from some old historical documents and predictions, just the year in which the great mundane show would break up. When I was a small boy at school in the early forties, during the Millerite excitement about the approaching end of all mundane things, I remember, on the day when the momentous event was expected to take place, how the larger school-girls were thrown into a great state of alarm and agitation by a thundercloud that let down a curtain of rain, blotting out the mountain on the opposite side of the valley.

"There it comes!" they said, and their tears flowed copiously. I remember that I did not share their fears, but watched the cloud, curious as to what the end of the world would be like. I cannot brag, as Thoreau did, when he said he would not go around the corner to see the world blow up. I am quite sure my curiosity would get the better of me and that I should go, even at this late day. Or think of the more harmless obsession of many good people about the second coming of Christ, or about the resurrection of the physical body when the last trumpet shall sound. A little natural knowledge ought to be fatal to all such notions. Natural knowledge shows us how transient and insignificant we are, and how vast and everlasting the world is, which was aeons before we were, and will be other aeons after we are gone, yea, after the whole race of man is gone. Natural knowledge takes the conceit out of us, and is the sure antidote to all our petty anthropomorphic views of the universe.

꩜ V

I was struck by this passage in one of the recently published letters of Saint-Gaudens: "The principal thought in my life is that we are on a planet going no one knows where, probably to something higher (on the Darwinian principle of evolution); that, whatever it is, the passage is terribly sad and tragic, and to bear up at times against what seems to be the Great Power that is over us, the practice of love, charity, and courage are the great things."

The "Great Power" that is over us does seem unmindful of us as individuals, if it does not seem positively against us, as Saint-Gaudens seemed to think it was.

Surely the ways of the Eternal are not as our ways. Our standards of prudence, of economy, of usefulness, of waste, of delay, of failure—how far off they seem from the scale upon which the universe is managed or deports itself! If the earth should be blown to pieces to-day, and all life instantly blotted out, would it not be just like what we know of the cosmic prodigality and indifference? Such appalling disregard of all human motives and ends bewilders us.

Of all the planets of our system probably only two or three are in a condition to sustain life. Mercury, the youngest of them all, is doubtless a dead world, with absolute zero on one side and a furnace temperature on the other. But what matters it? Whose loss or gain is it? Life seems only an incident in the universe, evidently not an end. It appears or it does not appear, and who shall say yea or nay? The asteroids at one time no doubt formed a planet between Mars and Jupiter. Some force which no adjective can describe or qualify blew it into fragments, and there, in its stead, is this swarm of huge rocks making their useless rounds in the light of the sun forever and ever. What matters it to the prodigal All? Bodies larger than our sun collide in the depths of space before our eyes with results so terrific that words cannot even hint them. The last of these collisions—of this "wreck of matter and crush of worlds"—reported itself to our planet in

February, 1901, when a star of the twelfth
magnitude suddenly blazed out as a star of
the first magnitude and then slowly faded.
It was the grand finale of the independent
existence of two enormous celestial bodies. They apparently ended in dust that
whirled away in the vast abyss of siderial
space, blown by the winds upon which
suns and systems drift as autumn leaves.
It would be quite in keeping with the ob-
served ways of the Eternal, if these bodies
had had worlds in their train, teeming with
life, which met the same fate as the central
colliding bodies.

Does not force as we know it in this
world go its own way with the same disregard of the precious thing we call life?
Such long and patient preparations for it,—
apparently the whole stellar system in
labor pains to bring it forth,—and yet held
so cheaply and indifferently in the end!
The small insect that just now alighted in
front of my jack-plane as I was dressing
a timber, and was reduced to a faint yel-
low stain upon the wood, is typical of the

fate of man before the unregarding and un-
swerving terrestrial and celestial forces.
The great wheels go round just the same
whether they are crushing the man or
crushing the corn for his bread. It is all one
to the Eternal. Flood, fire, wind, gravity,
are for us or against us indifferently. And
yet the earth is here, garlanded with the
seasons and riding in the celestial currents
like a ship in calm summer seas, and man
is here with all things under his feet. All
is well in our corner of the universe. The
great mill has made meal of our grist and
not of the miller. We have taken our chan-
ces and have won. More has been for us
than against us. During the little segment
of time that man has been upon the earth,
only one great calamity that might be called
cosmical has befallen it. The ice age of one
or two hundred thousand years was such a
calamity. But man survived it. The spring
came again, and life, the traveler, picked itself up and made a new start. But if he had
not survived it, if nothing had survived it,
the great procession would have gone on

just the same; the gods would have been just as well pleased.

The battle is to the strong, the race is to the fleet. This is the order of nature. No matter for the rest, for the weak, the slow, the unlucky, so that the fight is won, so that the race of man continues. You and I may fail and fall before our time; the end may be a tragedy or a comedy. What matters it? Only some one must succeed, will succeed.

We are here, I say, because, in the conflict of forces, the influences that made for life have been in the ascendant. This conflict of forces has been a part of the process of our development. We have been ground out as between an upper and a nether millstone, but we have squeezed through, we have actually arrived, and are all the better for the grinding—all those who have survived. But, alas for those whose lives went out in the crush! Maybe they often broke the force of the blow for us.

Nature is not benevolent; Nature is just, gives pound for pound, measure for measure, makes no exceptions, never tempers her decrees with mercy, or winks at any infringement of her laws. And in the end is not this best? Could the universe be run as a charity or a benevolent institution, or as a poor-house of the most approved pattern? Without this merciless justice, this irrefragable law, where should we have brought up long ago? It is a hard gospel; but rocks are hard too, yet they form the foundations of the hills.

Man introduces benevolence, mercy, altruism, into the world, and he pays the price in his added burdens; and he reaps his reward in the vast social and civic organizations that were impossible without these things.

I have no doubt that the life of man upon this planet will end, as all other forms of life will end. But the potential man will continue and does continue on other spheres. One cannot think of one part of the universe as producing man, and no other part as capable of it. The universe is all of a piece so far as its material constituents are concerned; that we know. Can there be any doubt that it is all of a piece so far as its invisible and intangible forces and capabilities are concerned? Can we believe that the earth is an alien and a stranger in the universe? that it has no near kin? that there is no tie of blood, so to speak, between it and the other planets and systems? Are the planets not all of one family, sitting around the same central source of warmth and life? And is not our system a member of a still larger family or tribe, and it of a still larger, all bound together by ties of consanguinity? Size is nothing, space is nothing. The worlds are only red corpuscles in the arteries of the infinite. If man has not yet appeared on the other planets, he will in time appear, and when he has disappeared from this globe, he will still continue elsewhere.

I do not say that he is the end and aim of creation; it would be logical, I think, to expect a still higher form. Man has been man but a little while comparatively, less than one hour of the twenty-four of the vast geologic day; a few hours more and he will be gone; less than another geologic day like the past, and no doubt all life from the earth will be gone. What then? The game will be played over and over again in other worlds, without approaching any nearer the final end than we are now. There is no final end, as there was no absolute beginning, and can be none with the infinite.